The BOY With No Name

Written by
Christopher Williams

To order additional copies of this book, contact:
Xlibris
1-888-795-4274
www.Xlibris.com
Orders@Xlibris.com

Once upon a time. In a land far far away. There was a small town with no name.

There lived a young boy with no name. All of his friends had no names. And his teacher had no name. His parents also had no names.

One day after walking home from school the boy with no name found a book.

And on this book there was a name. At first he was afraid because he had never seen a name. But he was also curious to see what was inside. He dare not let anyone see. So he took the book to a quiet place.

When the boy with no name open the book he was surprised to see there was another name inside. He stared at the names in the book for a long time. Then he began to believe he too could have a name.

So the young boy with no name closed his eyes really tight.
"I wish, I wish, I wish I too could have a name," the boy said.

Then a beautiful woman appeared. "Do not fear me," she said. When you wished upon the morning star, the star sent me to you. My name is Faith and, yes you too can have a name." "What do I have to do," the young no name asked? First you must truly believe. Then let everyone know that you seek a name. Take anyone with you who will go. Follow the Sun and never give up.

Remember even when you do not see me, I am always with you," the woman yelled as the boy ran home to tell his parents.

On his way home he saw his friends. He told them that he was going to get a name. "No way, you can never do that," one said. "That is stupid," said another. Some of his friends began to frown. "It is because you do not have Faith," the young boy said.

"You are all welcome to come and receive your own name," the boy with no name said. "We don't want to go to your stupid place," his friends teased.

And the boy with no name walked home with his head down.

At home the boy with no name told his parents that he was going to get a name. "Why do you want a name? Don't you love us?" his mother asked. "Do you think you are better than us?" his father asked. "I just want a name," the boy said.

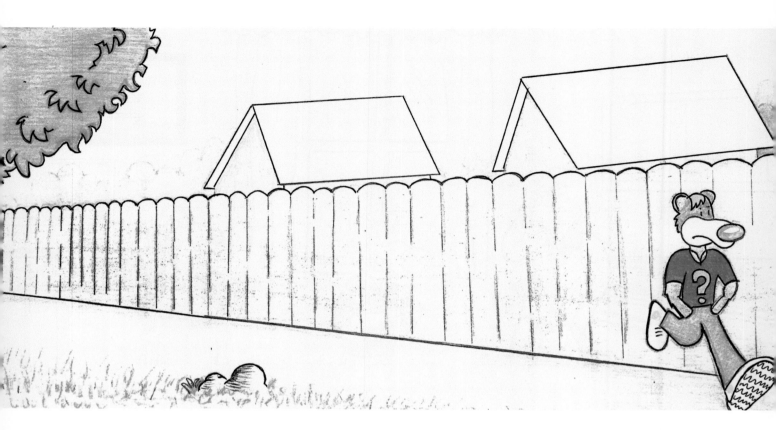

Without anyone to accompany him, the boy with no name began his journey.

The young no name came to the toll bridge at the edge of the town. There sat the mayor of No Name. And where do you think you are going little boy," the mayor asked. "I am going to get a name," the boy said. "But you are a no name. No names do not get names. Return home at once and stop with this nonsense," he snapped.

So the boy with no name followed the water looking
for another way to cross. The longer he walked the
farther the water stretched to the other side. He
walked and walked and walked.

Until he came to a man loading his boat with animals. "Excuse me sir, may I hitch a ride with you to the other side of the water?" the boy asked. "I am sorry my son my boat is full," the man said. "Do you have a name?" the boy asked. "Why ? Yes my name is Noah," the man said. And what is yours young sir?" Noah asked. "I am searching for my name."" Well I assure you keep Faith and you will find a great name."

15

So the boy with no name continued his journey. He walked and walk until he came to two pair of foot prints in the sand. So he followed them to the water where he only found one man staring out at the sea.

"Hello to you," the man said as he seen the young boy approaching. My name is Moses and you are?" Moses asked. "I am a no name from the land of No Name. I am searching for a name," the boy said. "Do you have faith?" Moses asked. "Yes," the boy replied.
"Then you will find a great name," Moses said. "I have been walking a long time and I cannot find the end of the sea. I must cross over to the other side to find my name."

So Moses lifted both his hands and the sea parted. "Your name will also be great," Moses said. Then the boy thanked Moses and continued on his journey.

He walked and walked and walked.

Until he became thirsty.

And then there was water.

And when he became hungry, he found an apple tree
in the middle of the desert.

When night came, he became scared of the shadows in the valley. But with faith he feared no evil.

Yet the next day he came to a sign in the middle of his path that read: Valley of the Giants.

When he saw the giant he wish he was back in No Name and he was lost without faith. When she appeared she asked, "why are you afraid was I not with you....

When you were thirsty did you not find water? And when you were hungry did you not find food?" "Yes," he said. "But the giant is powerful and I am but a boy." "Take these shall marbles and uses them to defeat the giant. Remember I am with you."

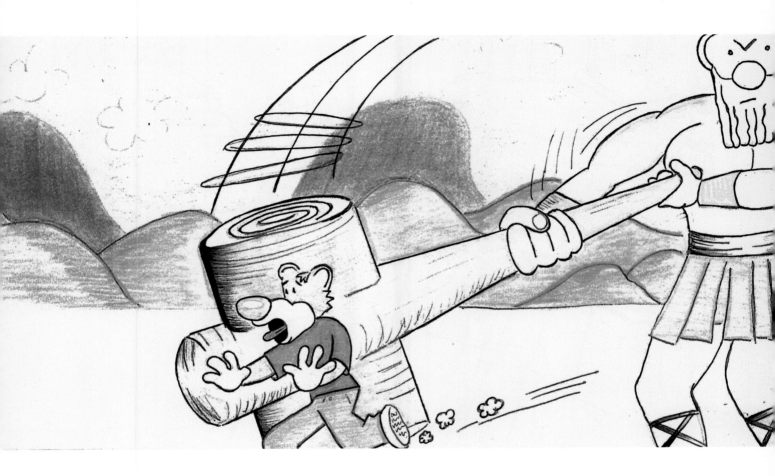

The young no name ran as fast as he could but he did not understand what Faith wanted him to do with the marbles.

When he reached the end of the road he had felt lost
and he did not know what way to go. He remembered
that Faith had always been with him.

The young no name closed his eyes really tight and pitched the marbles on the ground.

The giant was running so fast that he had slipped on the marbles and fell off the cliff.

After the young boy defeated the giant, Faith told him to walk to the water front. There he saw a bright light in the middle of the sea. But he did not know how he would get there.

With Faith the young no name knew that anything was possible so he walked across the water to the bright light.

In the light there was a man wearing white that told the boy with his new name he was very well pleased. "Now you must go home and show them your name. Your name is Forever and Ever."

The end

Printed in the United States
By Bookmasters